THE BIG HUG

Megan Walker

POW!

Brooklyn, NY

On opposite sides of a quiet street,

there lived two friends.

From morning to evening,
they played.

"You two are stuck together like glue!" their parents laughed.

And it was true.

They put their friendship into running
and climbing and jumping.

It was scraped knees and dirty clothes and only stopping to catch your breath.

Sometimes the fun would end and there would be tears and fights,

but they were always ready to give each other a big hug.

Then they would pick each other back up and start again.

Together they were a whirlwind of happiness.

So it was a shock when, one day,
they had to stop and go inside.

Between them now was only space.

Suddenly, outside was scary and felt very large. Their parents were full of whispers and frowns, and the worry inside felt heavy.

The two children felt alone, as if their friendship had slipped out the window, into the quiet where all their running and jumping and fun had gone missing.

Where can you put friendship when friends are apart?

Slowly, they learned.

They found that, across the street and through windows,
they could give each other a hug.

A smile
is a hug.

A wave
is a hug.

Soon they found that pictures in windows

and puppet shows

and dance competitions
were hugs too.

Laughter was a very good hug.

Sometimes their parents would help and the
new magic would spread to them as, for a short while,
their worries and whispers would disappear.

After some time, they could go outside.

They could see each other, their family and neighbors right there, without walls in between.

But still, they had to keep a distance.
During this strange way of living, however,
the two children had made a discovery.

They had discovered that when you're apart,
a friendship doesn't leave.

With time and effort a friendship will grow.

It can squeeze through bricks and reach over the sky and wait patiently for a long, long time.

A friendship is a hug when you can't be there.

Slowly, the days began

to feel less hard.

There were

fewer tears and

less bad news

and more smiles.

Everything began to feel lighter.

Until, finally,

they could be

together again

for one big…

hug.

Text and Illustrations © 2020 by Meghan Walker

Published by POW! a division of powerHouse Packaging & Supply, Inc.
32 Adams Street,
Brooklyn, NY 11201-1021

info@powkidsbooks.com
www.powkidsbooks.com
www.powerHouseBooks.com
www.powerHousePackaging.com

Printing and binding by Toppan Leefung
Book design by Robert Avellar

Library of Congress Control Number: 2020950795
ISBN: 978-1-57687-979-5
10 9 8 7 6 5 4 3 2 1

Printed in China

"For Ed and Isaac,
with lots of big hugs."
—M.W.

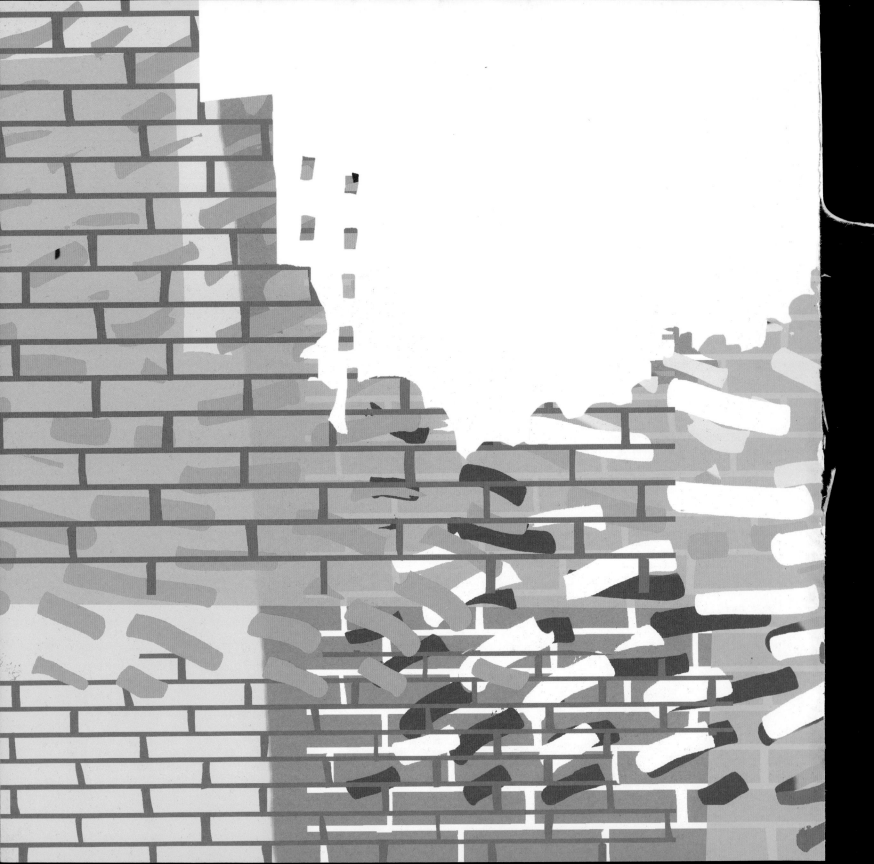